By **Evan Shine**

Illustrated by **Josh Holtsclaw**

A Random House PICTUREBACK® Book

Random House 🏠 New York

Materials and characters from the movie *Cars 2*. Copyright © 2011 Disney/Pixar. Disney/Pixar elements © Disney/Pixar, not including underlying vehicles owned by third parties; and, if applicable: Jeep® and the Jeep® grille design are registered trademarks of Chrysler LLC; Maserati logos and model designations are trademarks of Maserati S.p.A. and are used under license; Porsche is a trademark of Porsche; Volkswagen trademarks, design patents and copyrights are used with the approval of the owner, Volkswagen AG; Bentley is a trademark of Bentley Motors Limited; FIAT and Topolino are trademarks of FIAT S.p.A.; Background inspired by the Cadillac Ranch by Ant Farm (Lord, Michels and Marquez) © 1974. All rights reserved. Published in the United States by Random House Children's Books, a division of Random House, Inc., 1745 Broadway, New York, NY 10019, and in Canada by Random House of Canada Limited, Toronto, in conjunction with Disney Enterprises, Inc. Pictureback, Random House, and the Random House colophon are registered trademarks of Random House, Inc.

ISBN: 978-0-7364-2779-1
www.randomhouse.com/kids

Printed in the United States of America
10 9 8 7 6 5 4 3 2 1

Lightning McQueen was one happy race car. He had just won the biggest race in North America. Now he was home in Radiator Springs, celebrating with his girlfriend, Sally, and his best friend, Mater.

"Hey, listen up!" someone shouted. Lightning and Sally rolled indoors to see what all the excitement was about.

The international racing sensation, Francesco Bernoulli, was on TV: "Francesco is so superior to Lightning McQueen, it's funny!" the cocky racer boasted. Then Lightning heard Mater call the talk show to defend his friend!

When Francesco insulted Mater,
Lightning's jaw dropped. *Francesco
was making fun of his best buddy!*

Lightning told Francesco **the race was on!**

"I can't believe I entered that race, Mater," Lightning complained to the tow truck. "I really did want to spend time with Sally."

"You're gonna beat that **fancy-dancy** Francesco," Mater said. He believed in Lightning—and was proud to be the red race car's best friend.

"I got this dent when you was stuck in that ditch over there. It's a sign of friendship! And this one—"

But Lightning was hardly listening to Mater. He was thinking about beating Francesco in the World Grand Prix!

The next day, Sally drove to the airport to wish Lightning **good luck**.

"Show that handsome Francesco you're the fastest racer in the world," Sally said.

"I might just do that," Lightning replied, smiling.

The first race of the World Grand Prix was in Japan. When the
race began, Lightning took the lead! Then he heard Mater over
the headphones telling him to turn right. Lightning swerved right.
Francesco spun past him, winning the race.

"Ha-ha! Francesco has won, as predicted!" Francesco boasted.

"MATER, WHY DID YOU DO THAT?"

Lightning shouted.

"I didn't mean to make you lose," Mater replied sadly.

Later that day, Lightning discovered that Mater had flown home. *Now I can focus on beating Francesco,* Lightning thought.

Soon the racers were off to Italy for the second international race. Lightning's pit crew spent a day visiting Luigi's hometown.

Uncle Topolino told Lightning that Guido and Luigi always used to fight, but always made up in the end. "You gotta stand by your friends."

As it grew darker, Lightning
slipped away to be by himself. He
wandered the back roads and found some
tractors, but decided it would be no fun to tip
them without Mater. He looked up at the stars,
but they weren't romantic without Sally.

Finally, Lightning found a long, twisting dirt road.
Just like Willy's Butte back home, he thought. Lightning
pushed himself to the limit around the curves.

Then he spun out . . . right into a ditch. HE WAS STUCK!

If Mater were here, he could tow me out, Lightning thought. Luckily, he saw some headlights approaching. Was it Mater?

"Hey, buddy!" Lightning shouted. "Over here! I could sure use a tow!"

But it wasn't Mater—it was Uncle Topolino!

As Uncle Topolino helped Lightning out of the ditch, he accidentally dented the red race car.

"It's okay!" Lightning said, thinking back to what Mater had told him. "Dents mean we're friends."

"Good. This is good," Uncle Topolino replied.

The next day, the race in Italy was about to begin.

"Where is the rusty, **dented** truck?" Francesco
asked Lightning.

"Uh, well . . . ," Lightning said. "I messed up,
and he went home."

swoosh!

The starting flag went down, and Lightning raced harder than ever. He did it for Mater. And when Lightning won, he realized that he had something Francesco didn't— friends. Good friends, like Mater and Sally, who would always believe in him, no matter what.

In England, Mater finally showed up.

"Mater! Gee, it's good to see you!" Lightning said.

"We're still best buddies, right?" Mater asked.

"Absolutely!" Lightning replied with a grin. "And I'm sorry, Mater." Then he got an idea.

THE RACE OF THE CENTURY

LIGHTNING McQUEEN

VS

FRANCESCO

"How about racing in Radiator Springs?" Lightning asked Francesco. "It's the best way to find out who really is the fastest car in the world."

"Francesco is the fastest!" Francesco said as he flashed a smile. **The race was on!**

Lightning was happy to get home to Radiator
Springs. He went to see Sally right away.
Sally spotted his new dent. "Nice addition
to the best-looking and sweetest race car in the

At the same time, Mater was pulling Francesco from a ditch out at Willy's Butte.

"Ah, ow!" Francesco yelped.

"You got a **dent**? Hey, I guess we're all friends now!" Mater said, delighted.

The next day, the stands in the Radiator Springs stadium were filled. When the flag went down, Lightning and Francesco took off.

"*Ka-ciao*, Francesco!" Lightning shouted as the two cars began their race—and their friendship—dents and all.